RAINBOW magic ®

The Pet Keeper Fairies

For Tom Powell, with lots of love

Special thanks to
Sue Mongredien

ORCHARD BOOKS
338 Euston Road, London NW1 3BH
Orchard Books Australia
Hachette Children's Books
Level 17/207 Kent Street, Sydney, NSW 2000
A Paperback Original

First published in Great Britain in 2006
Rainbow Magic is a registered trademark of Working Partners Limited.
Series created by Working Partners Limited, London W6 0QT

ISBN 1 84616 168 1
1 3 5 7 9 10 8 6 4 2

Printed and bound in China

Georgia the Guinea Pig Fairy

by Daisy Meadows

illustrated by Georgie Ripper

ORCHARD BOOKS

www.rainbowmagic.co.uk

Fairies with their pets I see
And yet no pet has chosen me!
So I will get some of my own
To share my perfect frosty home.

This spell I cast. Its aim is clear:
To bring the magic pets straight here.
Pet Keeper Fairies soon will see
Their seven pets living with me!

Contents

Farmyard Fun

"This must be one of the cutest animals in the whole of Strawberry Farm!" Rachel Walker declared, her eyes shining. She stroked the woolly lamb in her arms. "He's so cuddly!"

"And hungry, too," her best friend, Kirsty Tate, chuckled. She tilted up the bottle of milk she was holding to feed

the lamb, under the watchful eye of
a farmhand. "He's nearly finished
this already!"

"He's making me thirsty, just
watching him!" her mum said, as the
lamb drained the last few drops.

Rachel was staying with Kirsty's family for a week over the Easter holidays. This afternoon, they were having a great time at Strawberry Farm. They had already seen a troop of tiny ducklings venturing out for their first swim on the pond, and enjoyed a pony ride on a sturdy little brown Shetland called Conker. Then, when a farmhand had announced that he wanted some volunteers to help him hand-feed some of the lambs, Rachel and Kirsty had jumped at the chance!

Rachel put the lamb down carefully, and both girls watched him gambol off to join the other lambs in the field.

"I saw a sign for 'Pets' Corner' over there," Rachel said, with a meaningful look at Kirsty. "Shall we go there next?" Kirsty smiled at her friend, picking up on Rachel's message at once. The two girls shared a wonderful secret: they'd been helping the Pet Keeper Fairies of Fairyland all week! Nasty Jack Frost had kidnapped the Pet Fairies' seven magical pets and had taken them all to his ice castle. But the pets had managed to escape, and make their way into the human world. Yesterday, Rachel and Kirsty had helped Bella the Bunny

Fairy find her lost rabbit. And the day before they'd reunited Katie the Kitten Fairy with her missing kitten. So Kirsty knew exactly what Rachel was hoping: perhaps they'd find another magical pet today in the Pets' Corner!

"Sounds lovely, but I think I'll opt out and go for a coffee," Mrs Tate said. "Shall I meet you both back here at four o'clock?"

"Good idea," Kirsty replied, trying not to sound too enthusiastic. Much as she loved her mum, she and Rachel always had their very best adventures when they were alone! "See you later."

Mrs Tate went towards the tea room, and the two friends headed for Pets' Corner.

"Here we are," Rachel said as they entered an area surrounded by a small fence. "Keep your eyes peeled for any magical pets who might be here!" she added in an excited whisper.

The girls began looking at all the rabbits and guinea pigs in their hutches and runs. Every animal had a little sign outside its cage, telling visitors its name and favourite food.

"Ahh, this rabbit is called Albie, and he likes carrot tops and brussel sprout peelings," Kirsty read aloud, peeping in at the fluffy grey rabbit. "Hello, Albie!"

"Rosie the guinea pig likes sunflower seeds and lettuce leaves," Rachel read, further along the row of hutches. "Millie, her sister, likes sliced apple. And Carrot, Rosie's baby, likes carrots... Oh!"

ROSIE, MILLIE & CARROT
Rosie likes sunflower seeds and lettuce leaves. Millie, her sister likes sliced apple, and Carrot, Rosie's baby, likes carrots and banana skins

Kirsty looked up. "What's wrong?" she asked.

Rachel was crouching down and peering into one of the runs. "There are supposed to be three guinea pigs in here – Millie, Rosie and baby Carrot," she told Kirsty. "But the baby guinea pig is missing!"

ROSIE, MILLIE & CARROT
Rosie likes sunflower seeds and lettuce leaves. Millie, her sister, likes sliced apple and Carrot, Rosie's baby, likes carrots and banana sk...

Kirsty hurried over. "Oh, dear, look," she said. "The cage door's open a crack – Carrot must have escaped!"

Out of the corner of her eye, Rachel

suddenly spotted a flash of fur behind the
hutches. She turned to see
a small orange and white
guinea pig squeezing
under the wooden fence.
"That must be Carrot
over there," she cried.

Kirsty fixed the cage door firmly shut,
then jumped up to look. "Oh, no — he's
heading for that field of sheep!" she
said, pointing.

Rachel looked anxious and headed off
after the little guinea pig. "He's too
young to be out on his own," she said.
"We've got to rescue him, Kirsty!"

Magic in Mid-Air!

Kirsty and Rachel clambered over the wooden fence surrounding the field of sheep and hurried after the guinea pig, who was now scampering busily towards a tree on the far side of the field. But both girls stopped and stared in disbelief when the guinea pig reached the base of the tree, for instead

of stopping, or swerving around the
tree, the little animal simply ran
straight on up the trunk!

"I didn't think guinea
pigs could do that!"
Kirsty gasped. "I'll
go after him, in
case he gets stuck."
Kirsty clambered
up into the tree
and picked her
way from branch
to branch until
she was within
arm's reach
of the little
guinea pig, who
was watching
her curiously.

"Hello," Kirsty said in a soft voice, reaching out towards him. As she did so, the guinea pig twitched his nose and backed away playfully.

Kirsty stretched out her hand a little further. "Come here, little Carrot," she said coaxingly. Again the guinea pig backed away, and Kirsty thought she glimpsed a whiskery little smile on his face as he did so!

"I'm imagining things now," Kirsty said to herself. She inched a little further along the branch and then leaned out in an effort to reach the guinea pig. Just as her fingertips were about to touch Carrot's fur, he jumped right off the branch…and scampered merrily away through the air!

Kirsty nearly fell out of the tree in surprise. "Rachel, look!" she cried excitedly, scrambling back down to the ground.

Rachel felt a delicious thrill of
excitement as she realised what was
happening. "That's not Carrot, the
farm guinea pig," she laughed. "It must
be Georgia the Guinea Pig Fairy's
magic pet!" She and Kirsty had met all
the Pet Keeper Fairies in Fairyland.
"I wonder where Georgia is."

At that very moment, the girls
suddenly heard the sound of
cheerful singing above
them, and looked up
to see Georgia herself
swooping towards
them on the back
of a blackbird.

"Georgia!" Rachel
cried, waving at
the pretty fairy.

Georgia waved back cheerily as the blackbird perched near the girls on a branch of the tree. She had short black hair and she wore a tan-coloured top and suede skirt, both edged with a fringe of turquoise beads and tassels. She smiled as she slipped off the blackbird's back and thanked him for the ride. The blackbird chirruped a merry reply and fluttered away.

Georgia flew over to Rachel's shoulder, her gauzy wings shimmering in the sunlight. "Hello, girls," she said, in a clear, silvery voice.

"We were looking for a lost guinea pig called Carrot," Kirsty explained eagerly. "But we found your magic pet instead, Georgia!"

Georgia twirled in mid-air excitedly when she heard that. "I thought he was somewhere near here!" she declared, looking around. "Oh, Sparky, hello!" she called, seeing the little orange and white guinea pig trotting along in mid-air. "I've missed you so much!"

Rachel smiled as Sparky squeaked
joyfully in reply to
his fairy owner and
began scampering
towards her.
Meanwhile, the
little fairy was
listening to
Sparky's eager
squeaks. "He says
that he's been looking for Carrot, too,"
she told the girls. "And—"

But before Georgia could translate
any more of Sparky's message, one of
the sheep who'd been grazing nearby
suddenly leaped up on its hind legs. To
everybody's amazement, the sheep then
produced a butterfly net, swept it
through the air and captured Sparky!

"Hey!" Kirsty yelled. "What's going on?"

"That's not a sheep," Rachel called out in horror, seeing a long green nose poking out from the creature's woolly face. "It's a goblin in disguise!"

Goblins Undercover

A gleeful cackle floated through the air as the goblin ran across the field with Sparky trapped in the butterfly net.

"Oh, no!" Kirsty cried. "What are we going to do now?"

"I'll turn you into fairies so we can all fly after him," Georgia said quickly, waving her wand over the girls.

A stream of glittering turquoise sparkles
swirled out from the tip of her wand
and whirled around Kirsty and Rachel.
In an instant, both girls shrank down
to become tiny fairies.

Rachel fluttered her
shimmering wings,
enjoying the feeling
of being as light as air
as she floated off the
ground. Being a fairy
was just about the best thing

in the whole world,
but now the girls
had work to do!
"Let's follow that
sneaky goblin!"
she cried, zooming
through the air after him.

"Don't worry, Sparky, we're coming!"
Kirsty added, following Rachel.

But as they flew over the field of
sheep, several more sheep jumped up on
their back legs and began swiping at
Kirsty, Rachel and Georgia. More
goblins in sheep disguises!

"Now they're chasing us!" Rachel
warned, looking back over her shoulder
to see the goblins racing after them
with butterfly nets in their hands and
nasty grins on their faces.

"Fly higher," Georgia urged the girls.
"Don't let them catch you, too!"

Kirsty, Rachel and Georgia
flew up out of reach of the
goblins as they chased
after the one who'd
caught Sparky.
He ran into a big
old barn, and
they all zoomed
in after him.

It was very dark
inside the barn, and
at first the three friends
couldn't see very much
in the gloom. But then
Georgia muttered a few
magic words and the turquoise
tip of her wand suddenly glowed

brightly, like a glittering blue torch. "Sparky, where are you?" she called softly, fluttering over a stack of hay bales to look behind them. Kirsty and Rachel were also flying around the barn, hoping to catch a glimpse of the guinea pig. Suddenly, Sparky gave a couple of high-pitched squeaks, and Kirsty, Rachel and Georgia flew towards the sound at once. The magic pet's squeaks seemed to be coming from somewhere near the barn door.

Unfortunately, just as the girls and Georgia approached the door, the other goblins ran into the barn, and cheered with delight to see the three fairies hovering in front of them, caught off-guard.

"Catch them!" one of the goblins urged, swinging his net around in an attempt to scoop up the fairies.

"Oh, no, you don't!" Georgia cried, as she and the girls soared upwards away from the goblins.

Kirsty managed to dodge one goblin who made a grab for her, but the tallest goblin of all now had her in his sights. As Kirsty flew up, the goblin swished his butterfly net down – and Kirsty was caught in its mesh!

"Help!" she cried, beating her wings frantically as she tried to fly free.

"Ha!" the tall goblin smirked, putting a warty green hand over the top of the net. "You're my prisoner now!"

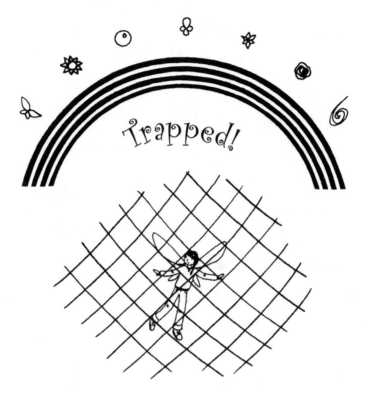

Trapped!

Georgia grabbed Rachel's hand and
pulled her up to a small, broken
window above the barn door, just as
the goblins swung the door shut with
a thump.

"What are we going to do?" Rachel
asked Georgia, her heart beating wildly
as they squeezed through the hole in

the window.
"The goblins
are holding
Kirsty prisoner!"
Georgia's eyes
were stormy.
"Don't worry, we'll
free her," she vowed.

"We need to think of a way to rescue
Kirsty and Sparky fast!"

Rachel and Georgia fell silent as they
both thought hard. They could hear the
goblins chortling triumphantly inside
the barn.

"A guinea pig and a fairy," one of
them crowed. "What a haul!"

"Jack Frost is going to be really
pleased with us today," another added,
sounding smug.

Then Rachel and Georgia heard
a scraping noise as the goblins slid
the bolt across the barn door.

"We'll sit tight until those other two
fairies have gone," a goblin muttered.
"Then we'll take this fairy and the
guinea pig back to Jack Frost's castle."

Rachel thought it was horrible to
hear the goblins gloating. She perched
on the window frame, racking her
brain. "Georgia, do you
think Sparky might
be able to magic
himself into
an elephant or
something, and
charge the door
down?" she suggested
after a few moments.

39

Georgia shook her head vigorously. "Sparky won't be able to use any magic," she told Rachel. "None of the magic pets can when they're afraid." She frowned in concentration. "We'll have to make the goblins want to leave the barn somehow," she went on. "Maybe we could tempt them out with something nice to eat?"

Rachel grinned as a brilliant idea suddenly popped into her head. "Or we could scare them out," she said eagerly. "Georgia, do you think you would be able to magic up the sound of an angry bull?"

"Of course," Georgia replied. Then she beamed as she realised what Rachel was plotting. "Of course, the sound of an angry bull who's just been woken

up by noisy goblins will be just the
thing to drive those goblins out of
the barn!" she whispered with a
mischievous chuckle.

Rachel nodded happily. "The barn is
so dark that the goblins will never
know that it's only fairy magic they
can hear," she added.

Georgia and Rachel grinned at
each other, and fluttered down to
the ground.

"Let's give it a try," Georgia said. "The sooner we free Kirsty and Sparky, the sooner we can find little Carrot."

She waved her wand, sending more turquoise sparkles swirling around Rachel. As soon as the magic fell upon her, Rachel grew back to her usual size.

Then Georgia pointed her wand at the barn doors and they shimmered for a few seconds with a magical turquoise light. "There," she whispered to Rachel. "I've used magic to hold the door shut, so even if the goblins unbolt it, they won't be able to come out until we let them."

Rachel smiled. "And we'll only let them out when they promise to hand over Kirsty and Sparky," she whispered back. "Brilliant, Georgia!" Then, with a wink at the smiling fairy, Rachel raised her voice. "Beware of the bull?" she said, as if she were reading aloud from a sign. "I wonder if those goblins know they're stuck in the barn with Farmer Tom's mean old bull. Phew!

He's a bad-tempered creature, way too crazy to be out in the fields." She laughed loudly. "I wouldn't like to be in there if the bull wakes up!"

Rachel glanced up at Georgia, who was now hovering outside the window above the barn door. With a wave of her wand, the little fairy sent a stream of magic all the way into the darkest corner of the barn.

Snort! Grunt! CRASH! A terrible
grunting and bellowing started up
where Georgia's magic had landed,
complete with a thunderous
hoof-stamping sound.

Georgia flew back
down to perch on
Rachel's shoulder,
trying not to laugh
out loud at their
clever trick.

Rachel pressed her ear
to the barn door to listen to the goblins.

"Whose stupid idea was it to come
in here anyway?" one of them hissed
nervously.

"Farmer Tom's crazy b-b-bull
sounds really a-a-angry!" another
goblin stuttered.

Rachel and Georgia heard the sound
of the bolt being pulled back, and then
one of the goblins tried to push the door
open, but, of course, Georgia's magic
was holding the door firmly shut.

"You're trapped in there," Rachel
couldn't resist telling the goblins, "with
Farmer Tom's mad bull!"

"Maybe the bull will make a nice pet
for Jack Frost," Georgia
suggested sweetly.

"Hey, let us out
right now!" a
goblin demanded,
thumping on
the door.

"I don't think
so," Georgia replied
in her silvery fairy voice.

Then, she zoomed up to the window
and waved her wand
again, sending more
magic into the barn.
Immediately, the
ferocious bellowing
of an angry bull started
up inside, but this time it
sounded even more bad-tempered.

"Oh, dear, all that shouting seems to
have made the bull even angrier!"
Georgia remarked sorrowfully.

The goblins hammered wildly on the
door in panic. "Let us out right now!"
they chorused.

Girls and Goblins Agree

"You let Kirsty and Sparky go, and then we'll let you out of the barn!" Rachel shouted to the goblins.

There was a moment's silence. "We can't go back to Jack Frost and say we've let another of those pesky pets slip through our fingers," Rachel heard a goblin whisper.

"First we messed up the kitten kidnap, then we bungled the bunny bagging. If we come back today without the guinea pig—"

"We can't go back without the guinea pig," another goblin interrupted. "But how about if we…"

Rachel pressed her ear as close to the barn door as possible, but the sneaky goblins were talking so quietly now that she couldn't hear what they were plotting.

"The fairy can go, but the guinea pig's staying with us!" a goblin voice announced after a moment.

Rachel looked at Georgia in dismay. She hadn't been expecting that response. "What shall we say?" she whispered.

"Let's agree, and then at least we know Kirsty's safe," Georgia replied. "Perhaps one of you will be able to grab Sparky as the goblins come out of the barn?"

Rachel nodded. "OK," she hissed. Then she turned back to the barn door.

"It's a deal," she shouted to the goblins. "Set Kirsty free!"

There was an anxious moment or two as Rachel and Georgia waited to see if the goblins were plotting a trick of their own, but then Kirsty zoomed out of the window and flew down to join them, smiling with relief.

Georgia waved her wand and turned Kirsty back into a girl.

Rachel hugged her tightly. "Are you all right? Were they mean to you and Sparky?" she asked.

"I'm fine," Kirsty said. "And so is Sparky. He's being very quiet, but he isn't hurt."

A peevish knocking came from the other side of the barn door. "A deal's a deal," one of the goblins yelled. "Open up before this crazy bull finds us."

Georgia pointed her wand at the doors.

"Now, we're going to try and grab the goblin who's got Sparky, OK?" Rachel whispered to Kirsty.

Kirsty nodded. "He was standing behind the others, at the back," she told Rachel quietly. "Ready when you are, Georgia."

Georgia waved her wand. The barn doors glittered with bright blue light again and then burst open. The goblins immediately raced out of the barn.

"Quick! Before the bull starts chasing us!" one of them shrieked.

Kirsty and Rachel made a lunge for the last goblin who was clutching Sparky, but their hands closed around empty air as he dodged them nimbly and sprinted away across the field.

"He's getting away!" cried Rachel in despair.

Kirsty looked around frantically for something she could use to stop the goblin.

Suddenly, she spotted an old coil of
rope just inside the barn. "Georgia,
could you magic that rope into a lasso
for me?" she asked quickly.

"Yes," the fairy replied, waving her
wand in a pattern
that sent turquoise
fairy dust
spiralling
along the
length of
the rope.
The frayed
old rope
immediately
turned into
a lasso and
flew straight up
into Kirsty's hand.

Kirsty swung the loop of the lasso around her head, keeping her eyes firmly fixed on the goblin who had Sparky. Then she launched the lasso straight at him.

The girls held their breath as the lasso flew through the air. It seemed to be heading a little wide, but Georgia quickly pointed her wand at it, and the lasso shone with blue magic and veered back on course towards the goblin. The loop of rope fell right over the goblin's head and caught tight around his middle, pinning his arms by his sides.

The goblin tried to keep running, but the rope pulled itself magically out of Kirsty's hands and wound itself around the goblin's legs, until he had to stop.

"Got him!" Kirsty cheered jubilantly.

Odd One Out

"Help!" the lassoed goblin yelled to his friends, but they were all far too busy running away from the imaginary bull to notice.

Rachel and Kirsty walked calmly over to the struggling goblin. Sparky, who was still in the goblin's hands, squeaked a welcome.

"Come here, Sparky,"
Rachel said, gently
lifting him out of
the goblin's fingers.

Sparky squeaked
even louder when he
saw Georgia fluttering in mid-air, and
with a twitch of his nose, he jumped
up towards her. As he was leaping
through the air, he shrank to his usual
tiny size and Georgia picked him up
happily for a cuddle.

"Hey! What about me?" the goblin shouted crossly, still tangled in the rope.

Georgia smiled at him. "Don't worry, the magic will wear off the lasso soon," she assured him. "In a couple of hours, or so, you'll be free..."

"A couple of hours?" the goblin groaned.

Georgia winked at Kirsty and Rachel as they began making their way back towards Pets' Corner. "It will only be a couple of minutes, really," she whispered, with a laugh.

Sparky started squeaking urgently, and suddenly Georgia looked worried. "Of course!" she cried. "We must find poor little Carrot! I'd almost forgotten about him."

Rachel looked at her watch. "It's a quarter to four already," she said. "Kirsty, we have to meet your mum in fifteen minutes. We don't have long to find Carrot."

"Then I'll turn you back into fairies," Georgia said, waving her wand briskly. "That way we can all fly around and look for him. Let's split up and meet back at Carrot's hutch in five minutes."

Fairy-sized once again, Rachel and Kirsty zoomed off in different directions, searching for the little, lost guinea pig. Kirsty checked out the play area, the cow barn and even popped through the windows of the gift shop, while Rachel hunted around the pig pen, the duck pond and the stables.

But there was no sign of Carrot anywhere.

"I don't understand it," Georgia said when they met up with her again five minutes later. "Where could he be?"

"We should go soon," Rachel said ruefully, "but I can't bear to leave the farm without knowing that Carrot's safe!"

Kirsty suddenly pointed ahead to where a mother hen was being followed by her line of chicks. "Wait a minute," she said, narrowing her eyes. "That's an odd looking chick at the end of the line!"

Rachel looked over to where Kirsty was pointing, and then giggled in relief. The last 'chick' in the line was not yellow and fluffy, like its fellows. It was a small, carrot-coloured guinea pig!

"Carrot's adopted a new family," Georgia chuckled. "How sweet!"

Sparky scampered over to Carrot and squeaked at him conversationally. Georgia, Rachel and Kirsty watched as Carrot looked at Sparky, then back at the chicks, as if he was working something out. Then he rubbed noses with Sparky and squeaked a reply.

Georgia grinned. "He says he's enjoyed being part of the hen family, but thinks he ought to go home now," she translated. "And we think so, too, little Carrot!"

Georgia checked that nobody else was in sight, then waved her wand over Rachel and Kirsty, turning them back into girls. Kirsty went over and picked up Carrot. "Come on," she said gently. "Let's take you back to your hutch."

As soon as Kirsty had placed Carrot back in his hutch, Rosie and Millie — Carrot's mum and aunt — rushed over and squeaked at Carrot excitedly. Then all three of them rubbed noses together, and Carrot nestled against Rosie, looking very content.

Georgia waved her wand to make sure that the cage door was tightly shut. "So there'll be no more going back to the hen house, OK?" she said to Carrot, with a smile.

Then she picked up Sparky, and turned to the girls. "It's nearly four o'clock, you'd better go," she told them. "And we should fly back to Fairyland, too, Sparky – where I'm going to make sure Jack Frost never gets anywhere near you again!"

Sparky nuzzled Georgia's arm and she stroked him gently. "Thank you for everything," she said to Kirsty and Rachel. "And Sparky says thank you, too."

Kirsty and Rachel hugged the tiny fairy goodbye, and gave Sparky a gentle stroke. Sparky squeaked goodbye to the girls, and then squeaked in the direction of Carrot's cage. A volley of squeaks came back in reply, as if the farm guinea pigs were calling out their goodbyes too.

And then, with
a burst of
turquoise sparkles
that fizzed and
glittered in the
afternoon sunlight,

Georgia and Sparky vanished.

Rachel and Kirsty watched as the air
rippled with a strange turquoise
shimmer and then was still once more.

"There you are, girls!" came a voice,
and Rachel and Kirsty turned

to see Mrs Tate walking
towards them. "Have
you had a nice day?"

"Great, thanks,
Mum," Kirsty
replied with a smile.
"Wasn't it, Rachel?"

"Oh, yes," Rachel agreed. She grinned broadly as she noticed a pot of sunflower seeds, some sliced apple and a whole pile of carrot sticks in the guinea pigs' cage. She felt sure the food was a gift from Georgia; it definitely hadn't been there before. "Today's been absolutely magic!" Rachel sighed happily.

The Pet Keeper Fairies

Georgia the Guinea Pig Fairy has got
her pet back. Now Rachel
and Kirsty must help

Lauren the Puppy Fairy

Win a Rainbow Magic
Sparkly T-Shirt and Goody Bag!

In every book in the Rainbow Magic Pet Keeper Fairies series (books 29-35) there is a hidden picture of a collar with a secret letter in it. Find all seven letters and re-arrange them to make a special Fairyland word, then send it to us. Each month we will put the entries into a draw and select one winner to receive a Rainbow Magic Sparkly T-shirt and Goody Bag!

Send your entry on a postcard to Rainbow Magic Pet Keeper Competition, Orchard Books, 338 Euston Road, London NW1 3BH. Australian readers should write to Hachette Children's Books, Level 17/207 Kent Street, Sydney, NSW 2000.
Don't forget to include your name and address.
Only one entry per child. Final draw: 30th April 2007.

Don't miss...
Kylie the Carnival Fairy

1-84616-175-4

Kylie the Carnival Fairy needs Kirsty's and Rachel's help! Jack Frost has stolen the three magic hats that make the Sunnydays Carnival so much fun, and the girls have to get them back...

Have you checked out the

website at:

www.rainbowmagic.co.uk

There are games, activities and fun things to do, as well as news and information about Rainbow Magic and all of the fairies.

by Daisy Meadows

The Rainbow Fairies

Ruby the Red Fairy	ISBN	1 84362 016 2
Amber the Orange Fairy	ISBN	1 84362 017 0
Saffron the Yellow Fairy	ISBN	1 84362 018 9
Fern the Green Fairy	ISBN	1 84362 019 7
Sky the Blue Fairy	ISBN	1 84362 020 0
Izzy the Indigo Fairy	ISBN	1 84362 021 9
Heather the Violet Fairy	ISBN	1 84362 022 7

The Weather Fairies

Crystal the Snow Fairy	ISBN	1 84362 633 0
Abigail the Breeze Fairy	ISBN	1 84362 634 9
Pearl the Cloud Fairy	ISBN	1 84362 635 7
Goldie the Sunshine Fairy	ISBN	1 84362 641 1
Evie the Mist Fairy	ISBN	1 84362 636 5
Storm the Lightning Fairy	ISBN	1 84362 637 3
Hayley the Rain Fairy	ISBN	1 84362 638 1

The Party Fairies

Cherry the Cake Fairy	ISBN	1 84362 818 X
Melodie the Music Fairy	ISBN	1 84362 819 8
Grace the Glitter Fairy	ISBN	1 84362 820 1
Honey the Sweet Fairy	ISBN	1 84362 821 X
Polly the Party Fun Fairy	ISBN	1 84362 822 8
Phoebe the Fashion Fairy	ISBN	1 84362 823 6
Jasmine the Present Fairy	ISBN	1 84362 824 4

The Jewel Fairies

The Pet Keeper Fairies

Look out for the Fun Day Fairies!

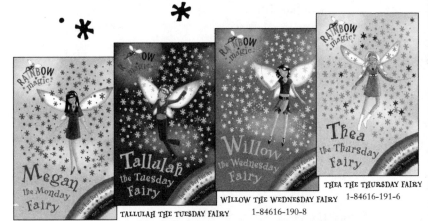

MEGAN THE MONDAY FAIRY
1-84616-188-6

TALLULAH THE TUESDAY FAIRY
1-84616-189-4

WILLOW THE WEDNESDAY FAIRY
1-84616-190-8

THEA THE THURSDAY FAIRY
1-84616-191-6

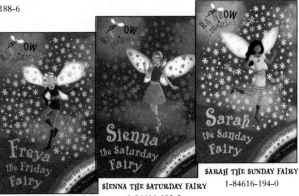

FREYA THE FRIDAY FAIRY
1-84616-192-4

SIENNA THE SATURDAY FAIRY
1-84616-193-2

SARAH THE SUNDAY FAIRY
1-84616-194-0

Available from
Saturday 2nd September 2006